Tiptoe Into SCARY CITIES

CREEPY
CHICAGO

by Krystyna Poray Goddu

Consultant: Debbie Felton
Professor of Classics
University of Massachusetts
Amherst, Massachusetts

BEARPORT
PUBLISHING

New York, New York

Credits

Publisher: Kenn Goin
Senior Editor: Joyce Tavolacci
Creative Director: Spencer Brinker
Photo Researcher: Thomas Persano
Cover: Kim Jones

Library of Congress Cataloging-in-Publication Data

Names: Goddu, Krystyna Poray, author.
 Title: Creepy Chicago / by Krystyna Poray Goddu.
 Description: New York : Bearport Publishing Company, Inc., 2019. | Series:
    Tiptoe into scary cities | Includes bibliographical references and index.
 Identifiers: LCCN 2018009291 (print) | LCCN 2018020646 (ebook) |
    ISBN 9781684027149 (Ebook) | ISBN 9781684026685 (library)
 Subjects: LCSH: Haunted places—Illinois—Chicago—Juvenile literature. |
    Ghosts—Illinois—Chicago—Juvenile literature.
 Classification: LCC BF1472.U6 (ebook) | LCC BF1472.U6 G625 2018 (print) | DDC
    133.109773/11—dc23
 LC record available at https://lccn.loc.gov/2018009291

For more information, write to Bearport Publishing Company, Inc., 45 West 21st Street, Suite 3B, New York, New York 10010. Printed in the United States of America.

10 9 8 7 6 5 4 3 2 1

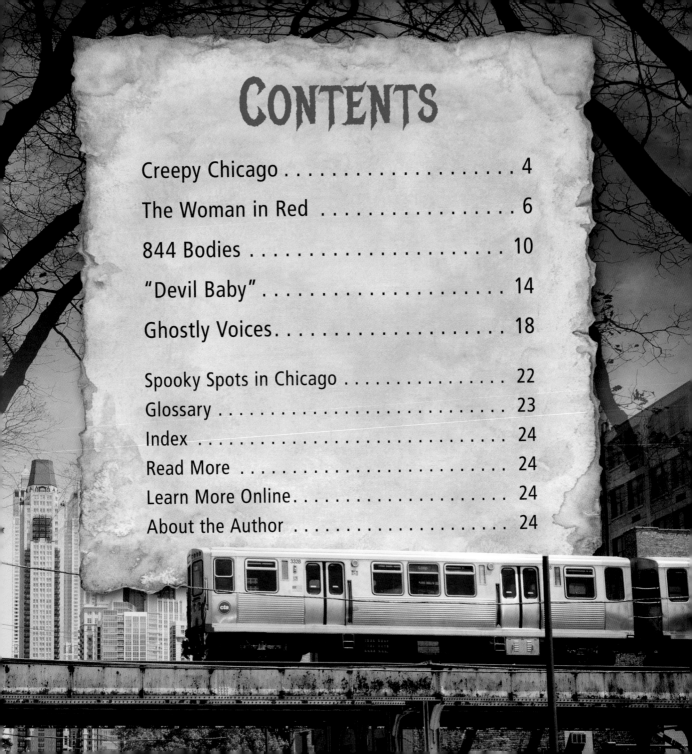

CONTENTS

CREEPY CHICAGO

A dark path curves along Lake Michigan. As you walk, a cold wind whips around you. It sends shivers down your spine. Mist rises from the lake. Suddenly, you feel you are not alone. Is somebody—or something—hiding in the mist?

Get ready to read four tales
about Chicago's spookiest
spots. Turn the page . . .
if you dare.

The Woman in Red

The Drake hotel

A terrified guest darted out of an elevator at The Drake hotel. What had scared her? A ghost!

The hotel guest had been in the elevator when it **jolted** to a stop. The doors opened at the tenth floor. A very pale woman in a blood-red gown appeared. She floated into the elevator like fog!

The Drake hotel in downtown Chicago

The Drake
hotel's lobby

7

Who is the Woman in Red? Travel back in time to 1920. There was a big party at the hotel. Couples twirled on the dance floor. A woman in red watched and smiled. Suddenly, her delight turned to **horror.** Her **fiancé** was kissing another woman!

Filled with anger, she took the elevator to the tenth floor. Then, she flung herself out a window to her death. Is this why her ghost still wanders the hotel?

In 1944, a woman named Adele Born Williams was shot dead at The Drake. Her ghost is also said to haunt the hotel.

Adele Born Williams

9

844 BODIES

Eastland disaster site, Chicago River

Every day, people pass by the Chicago River. Few know about the **disaster** that took place there. If you listen closely, you might still hear sobs, moans, and screams.

It was a misty morning in July 1915. Excited families boarded the *Eastland*, a steamship. More than 2,500 people crowded into the old ship.

The *Eastland* steamer

The families aboard the *Eastland* were headed to a picnic.

The Chicago River near the spot where people boarded the *Eastland*

11

As the *Eastland* pulled away from the **dock,** the run-down ship toppled over! Passengers were tossed into the river. "The screaming was the most horrible of all," remembers a nurse. In total, 844 people died in the accident. Twenty-two entire families drowned.

The *Eastland* after the accident

Even today, there are reports of ghostly cries near the disaster site. Screams and moans echo day and night. Will the **victims** ever rest?

Victims of the *Eastland* disaster

"Devil Baby"

Jane Addams Hull House

Jane Addams believed in helping others. In 1889, she opened Hull House in Chicago. There, she created a **community** for people in need. Everybody was welcomed. One day in 1912, a baby was left at the building. Yet there was something strange about the child.

Jane Addams

Hull House

15

The child is said to have had hooves, scaly skin, and a tail! Word spread about the "devil baby." Soon, people were banging on the doors to see it. Hull House workers claimed there was no such **demon** child. Yet thousands came to visit it. Was it real? No one will ever know.

The so-called devil baby became known around the country.

'DEVIL CHILD' STILL SOUGHT BY THOUSANDS

Ancient Superstition Spreads the Rumor of "Demon Baby" Over the City.

A thousand years from now an archaeologist will dig up a Chicago newspaper bearing the date "October 31, 1913." He will translate it, if its language is not too "dead" and then he will deliver a lecture in which will occur this paragraph:

It is a curious fact revealed by recent documentary discoveries that in the year 1913 the popular acceptance of impossible myths as truth was demonstrated precisely as it has been demonstrated in the years before men learned to count the centuries. People of North America only ten centuries ago were accepting as true a fable concerning the birth of a so-called "devil-baby" born...

A newspaper from 1912 telling of the devil baby

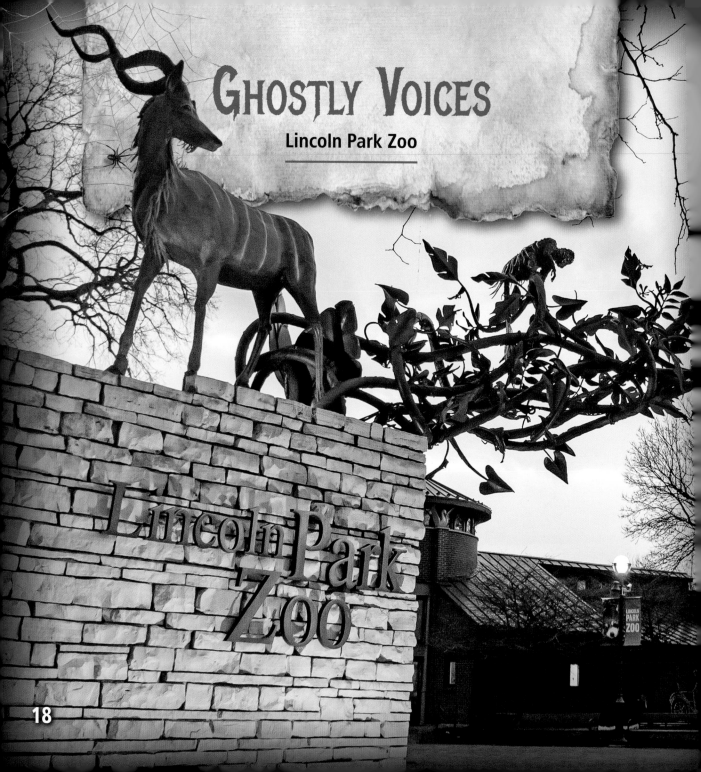

GHOSTLY VOICES

Lincoln Park Zoo

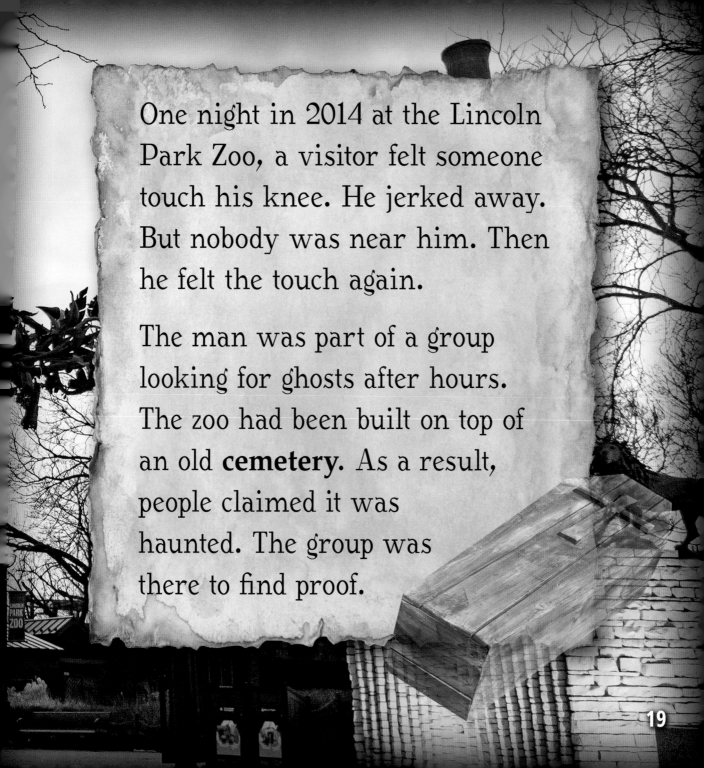

One night in 2014 at the Lincoln Park Zoo, a visitor felt someone touch his knee. He jerked away. But nobody was near him. Then he felt the touch again.

The man was part of a group looking for ghosts after hours. The zoo had been built on top of an old **cemetery**. As a result, people claimed it was haunted. The group was there to find proof.

After many hours, the group had not seen any ghosts. But they had brought along a voice recorder. When they listened to it later, they were shocked. **Shrieks** and laughter rang out. One voice dared: "Touch him!" And then another, "Touch him again!" At that moment, the man knew he had felt a ghost's hand on his knee.

More than 10,000 bodies are still buried under the Lincoln Park Zoo.

This building is a family tomb. It's the only part of the old cemetery that's still visible in the zoo.

Spooky Spots in Chicago

Eastland Disaster Site
Check out the scene of a deadly boat disaster.

Lincoln Park Zoo
Visit this historic zoo, built on top of an old cemetery.

Jane Addams Hull House
Was this the home of a devil baby?

The Drake Hotel
This hotel is home to several ghosts.

Lake Michigan

Chicago

CANADA

Pacific Ocean

ILLINOIS — Chicago

UNITED STATES

Atlantic Ocean

MEXICO

Gulf of Mexico

N
W   E
S

Glossary

cemetery (SEM-uh-ter-ee) an area of land where dead bodies are buried

community (kuh-MYOO-nuh-tee) a group of people who live together in the same place

demon (DEE-muhn) an evil spirit

disaster (dih-ZASS-tur) an event that causes terrible destruction

dock (DOK) an area where ships load and unload people or goods

fiancé (fee-AHN-say) a man who has promised to marry someone

horror (HOR-ur) strong fear

jolted (JOL-ted) moved suddenly with a jerk

shrieks (SHREEKS) loud, high-pitched cries

victims (VIK-tuhmz) people who have been hurt or killed

INDEX

READ MORE

Camisa, Kathryn. *Horror Hotels (Tiptoe Into Scary Places)*. New York: Bearport (2017).

Ramsey, Grace. *Haunted Hotels (Yikes! It's Haunted)*. Vero Beach, FL: Rourke (2017).

LEARN MORE ONLINE

To learn more about creepy Chicago, visit:
www.bearportpublishing.com/Tiptoe

ABOUT THE AUTHOR

Krystyna Poray Goddu is an author who lives in New York City. She loves visiting Chicago, but has not yet seen a ghost there.